This igloo book belongs to:

....

igloobooks

Published in 2019
by Igloo Books Ltd
Cottage Farm
Sywell
NN6 0BJ
www.igloobooks.com

Copyright © 2015 Igloo Books Ltd
Igloo Books is an imprint of Bonnier Books UK

GOL002 0519
4 6 8 10 11 9 7 5
ISBN: 978-1-70440-725-4

Written by Alice King
Illustrated by Lisa Alderson

Designed by Justine Ablett
Edited by Nicholas Oliver

Printed and manufactured in China

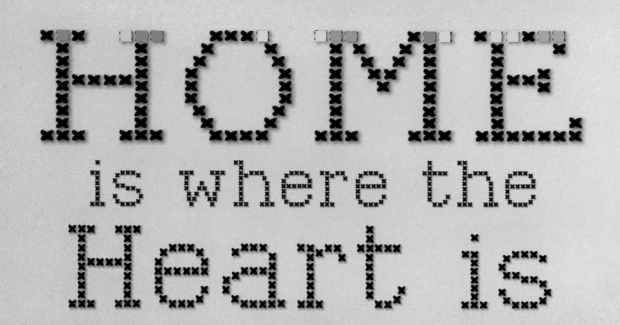

HOME
is where the
Heart is

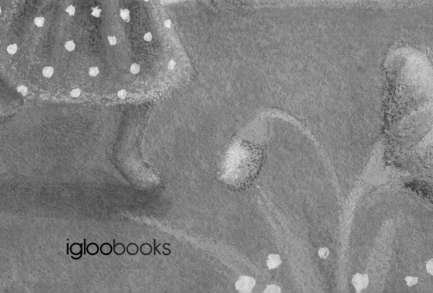

igloobooks

Home is where the heart is because it's the place to be. There are my two **cheeky** brothers, Mummy, Daddy and me.

Home means opening the curtains
on a **bright** and **sunny** day.

Gobbling breakfast down...

... and **running** outside to play.

Home is lots of hugs and lovely **squishy** cuddles.

Adventures

in the garden...

... and messy,

splashy

puddles.

Home is
making
dens...

... and having
fun inside.

Counting from **one** to **ten** and then **running** off to hide.

Home is cosy clothes...

... and **Shiny**

rainy day coats.

It's picnics in the garden...

... and **racing** sailing boats.

Home means **toasty,** roasty fires when the weather is cold.

Cuddling up and **snuggling,**
hoping stories will be told.

Home is all the **delicious** treats that clever Mummy makes.

It's **fun** birthday parties
and sugary, frosted cakes.

Home means tender hugs and tears that are quickly dried.

It means **kind** words that say,
"Don't cry now. At least you tried."

Home is a soft, warm bed and my **fluffy** teddy bear.

Sleeping through
the starlit night,
dreaming
without a care.

Home is where the **heart** is

because you are all there, too.

I just want you to know that
I really do love you.